This book
belongs to

_____

_____

First published in 2001 in Great Britain by

GULLANE
CHILDREN'S BOOKS

Winchester House, 259-269

Old Marylebone Road, London NW1 5XJ

1 3 5 7 9 10 8 6 4 2

Illustrations © Jane Cabrera 2001

The right of Jane Cabrera to be identified

as the illustrator of this work has been

asserted by her in accordance with the

Copyright, Designs, and Patents Act, 1988.

For Paula

A CIP record for this title is available

from the British Library.

ISBN 1-86233-340-8 hardback

ISBN 1-86233-304-1 paperback

Printed and bound in Hong Kong

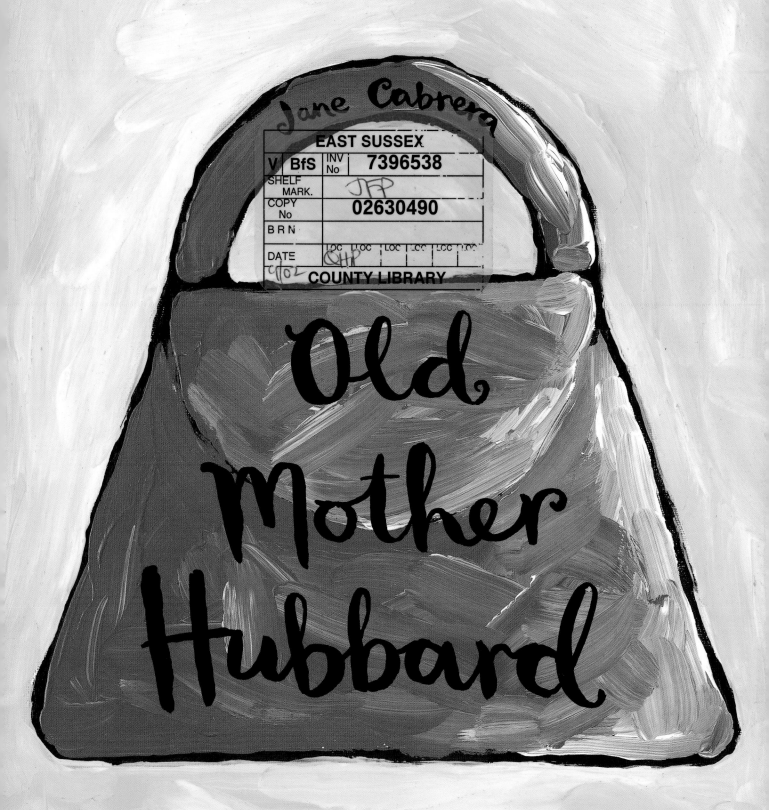

Jane Cabrera

Old Mother Hubbard

GULLANE
CHILDREN'S BOOKS

Old Mother Hubbard
went to the cupboard

But when she got there, the cupboard was bare, and so the poor dog had none

She went to the tailor's

to buy him a coat

But when she came back, he was riding a goat

She went to
the hatter's

to buy him
a hat

But when she came back, he was washing the cat

She went to
the barber's

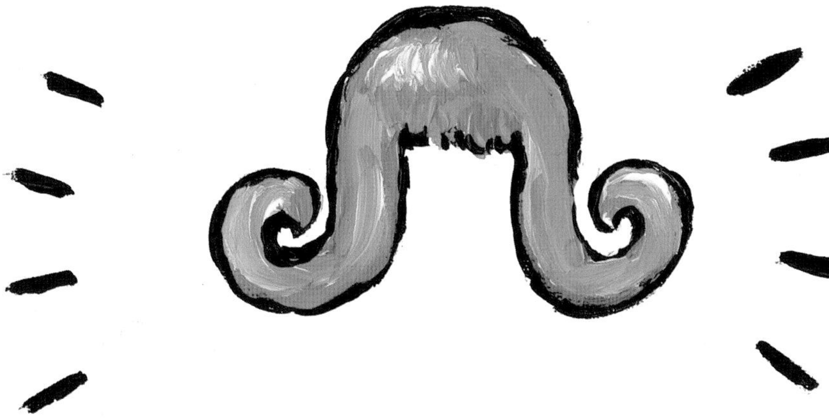

to buy him
a wig

She went to
the cobbler's

to buy him
some shoes

But when
she came back,
he was reading
the news

Then the dame made a curtsy,

The dog
made a bow

Domino

Jess

Tommy

Seal

Peggy

Max

EKKU

Other Gullane Picture Books for you to read:

Harry and the Bucketful of Dinosaurs
IAN WHYBROW • ADRIAN REYNOLDS

A Cuddle for Claude
DAVID WOJTOWYCZ

Yip! Snap! Yap!
CHARLES FUGE

Three Little Kittens
TANYA LINCH

Sometimes I Like to Curl up in a Ball
VICKI CHURCHILL • CHARLES FUGE

Little Ones Do!
JANA NOVOTNY HUNTER • SALLY ANNE LAMBERT

Not me!
NIGEL McMULLEN

GULLANE
CHILDREN'S BOOKS